SLAM DUNK
A Young Boy's Struggle
with Attention Deficit Disorder

by

Roberta N. Parker

Featuring

Commonly Asked Questions
About Attention Deficit Disorder

by

Harvey C. Parker, Ph.D.

Illustrations by
Richard A. DiMatteo

Impact Publications, Inc.
Plantation, Florida

To my family

Parker, Roberta N.
  Slam Dunk: A Young Boy's Struggle With
  Attention Deficit Disorder / by Roberta N. Parker

  p. 55

  Summary: A realistic story of a young boy's efforts
  to overcome problems associated with attention deficit
  disorder.

  ISBN 0-9621629-4-9

  1. Attention deficit disorder- Treatment-Juvenile literature
  2. Hyperactivity- Treatment -Juvenile literature

Published by Impact Publications, Inc. 300 NW 70th Avenue
Plantation, Florida 33317 (305) 792-8944.

Manufactured in the United States of America

10 9 8 7 6 5 4 3 2 1

CONTENTS

Resources

Other Books and Videos About Attention Deficit Disorders For Young Children and Teens

Gehret, Jeanne (1991). *Eagle Eyes.* New York. Verbal Images Press.

Goldstein, S. and Goldstein, M. (1991). *It's Just Attention Disorder: A Video For Kids.* Utah. Neurology, Learning and Behavior Center.

Gordon, M. (1991). *Jumpin' Johnny Get Back To Work!* New York. Gordon Publications, Inc.

Gordon, M. (1991). *My Brother's A World Class Pain.* New York. Gordon Publications, Inc.

Gordon, M. (1992). *I Would If I Could!* New York. Gordon Publications, Inc.

Levine, M. (1990). *Getting A Head In School. A Student's Book About Learning Abilities and Learning Disorders.* Massachusetts. Educator's Publishing Service.

Nadeau, K. and Dixon, E. (1991). *Learning To Slow Down and Pay Attention.* Virginia. Chesapeake Psychological Services.

Parker, Roberta. (1992). *Making the Grade: An Adolescent's Struggle with ADD.* Florida. Impact Publications, Inc.

Quinn, P. O. and Stern, J. M. (1991). *Putting On The Brakes. Young People's Guide To Understanding Attention Deficit Hyperactivity Disorder (ADHD).* New York. Magination Press.

All of the above products are available through the A.D.D.WareHouse. For more information about these and other products related to ADD, or to receive a free catalog call or write:

A.D.D. WareHouse, Inc.
300 Northwest 70th Avenue
Plantation, Florida 33317
(800) ADD-WARE • (305) 792-8944

Chapter One

Toby lied awake in bed and listened to the clatter of the trucks and buses and the chatter of the people on the street just below his bedroom window. The noises on the street became louder as the early morning sun filled his room with light. He woke up this way every morning. The sounds of the city streets were Toby's alarm clock.

Toby's mother worked as a nurse at a nearby hospital and had to leave for work very early in the morning so Toby, his older brother, Mike, and younger sister, May, were on their own in the morning. Since Toby was usually the first one to get up, his mother depended on him to wake his brother and sister for school.

This morning Mike and May were still asleep as usual. After Toby dressed, he would wake them. Not an easy thing to do since Mike liked to sleep and he often argued with Toby in the morning when Toby tried to get him up. Mornings were not Mike's favorite time, but once he got dressed he was okay and then he took charge of preparing breakfast.

May, on the other hand, was always sweet and

good-natured, even when she woke up early in the morning. Toby knew his mother depended on him to get his little sister ready for school.   He took this responsibility very seriously. After all, he was her big brother, even if Mike was the oldest.

After Mike, May and Toby finished eating break-fast, Mike, as always, reminded Toby to get his school books and papers ready and not to worry so much about May. Mike warned Toby, "May does just fine, so worry about yourself!"   Toby knew what that meant. Toby usually forgot to bring his lunch pass, pencils or impor-tant homework papers to school.

May, however, always knew just what she needed for school and she packed her book bag and got her school papers organized without much fuss. Even though Toby needed help himself, he felt good about checking on May. He always wanted to be there for her. After all, he was a third grader once himself.

While Toby got all his school supplies ready, Mike and May straightened up the kitchen. Then they each grabbed their books and left for school.

The three walked together for a block and then Mike turned up 95th Street towards Kennedy High School. Toby and May continued straight ahead for Liberty Grade School. Toby looked after May all the way there.

After getting May off to her class, Toby wandered to where a group of fifth grade boys were playing basketball in the school yard. The boys were passing the ball, dribbling and shooting hoops. Toby joined them. He loved basketball and hoped one day he would be a star player, just like Mike, over at Kennedy High.

Full of energy and eager to have a turn to shoot, Toby stood next to his classmate, Carl. Toby knew he was a pretty good shooter, especially from the foul line where he hardly ever missed. However, now it was someone else's turn. The ball hit the backboard, circled around the rim and bounced into Carl's hands. Toby grabbed the ball away from Carl, aimed for the basket and shot. The other kids yelled at him for going out of turn and not letting Carl take a turn to shoot. Toby didn't even notice their annoyance. All he could do was think about his shot, which went right in the basket. "Slam dunk!" Toby yelled, but nobody seemed too pleased with his accomplishment.

Carl scolded him, "Hey Toby, you cut ahead of me! Now the bell is ringing and we have to go to class. I missed my turn because of you!"

Toby felt badly, but there was no time to say he was sorry because there was no talking permitted as they filed in for class. He thought it over and realized that he should have let Carl have a shot instead of grabbing the ball away and shooting himself. Mike had always told him to slow down and not get so carried away. Mike was right. Toby wanted to slow down, but he just seemed to get so excited.

Mike didn't understand how easy it was to forget what to do. Neither did the guys in the school yard. The worst thing was that sometimes even his mother didn't understand.

Chapter Two

When school ended, May's class filed out of the building. As always, she searched for Toby so they could walk home together. Today she was particularly happy to see him and could hardly wait to tell him what a terrific day she had.

Toby was looking down at the ground and pouting. May was so excited about her own good feelings that she didn't notice. She had to tell Toby about her good fortune. She knew he would be so happy for her and so proud of her. Little did May know that Toby was so caught up with his own problems today, he couldn't give her a thought.

In his book bag Toby was carrying a letter for his mother. The letter was from his teacher, Mrs. Bolton. Toby knew his mother would be upset by a bad letter and he knew this one wasn't good, because Mrs. Bolton had been annoyed with him in class today.

May spoke excitedly, "Toby, my class is putting on a play and the teacher gave me a big speaking part. Isn't that great?"

Toby said nothing, so May repeated the news. He still didn't respond. She was shocked, so she asked him what was wrong.

He responded this time and said, "You blurted that out twice, May. Can't you control yourself?"

May felt disappointed. She had waited all afternoon just to share the news with Toby.

Toby started again, "Who cares about your silly old play, May?"

This time May got mad. She screamed, "Toby, you're the one who always interrupts and doesn't pay attention to others. Don't be mean to me! I'm always nice to you. I always put up with you when you check on me in the mornings. You're the one who is never ready on time!"

Toby was stunned. Checking on May in the

mornings always made him feel important. He thought of it as the one thing he did well. Now, he was hurt. May's words were painful to him. It was hard to think that she didn't need his help in the mornings.

When she saw the pain on his face she regretted what she had said, but it was too late. There was no way she could take it back. Without a word they walked down the street towards home.

After a few blocks, Toby broke the silence. He managed a strained smile and said, "May, I'm proud of you."

Then May asked, "Toby what's wrong? I'm sorry if I hurt you, but you're not acting like yourself today."

Toby spoke slowly and his voice quivered as he told May about the letter from his teacher. It was so hard to get the words out. If he could barely tell May, how would he ever be able to tell Mom?

May sensed his fear and reassured him that Mom loved him and even if she was angry, she wouldn't be angry forever. Toby knew May was just trying to make him feel better. This evening was going to be tough and he was scared.

Chapter Three

Toby spent a long time in his room before he gave his mother the letter from Mrs. Bolton. He tried to think of the perfect time to give it to her, but he could think of none. She was in the kitchen cooking dinner when he handed it to her. At first she thought it was just another notice from school, but as she read on she asked with disappointment, "Toby, what is this?"

Toby answered sadly, "Mom, I try to do my work and stay out of trouble, but I can't."

Mom read the letter aloud.

Dear Mrs. Butler,

I am writing this letter to keep you informed of Toby's work in school this year.

Although Toby is a smart young man he is having trouble paying attention in class and isn't finishing his work. He is easily distracted by others and has difficulty staying in his seat. I often have to remind him to write down assignments and to organize his papers.

Toby is in danger of failing several subjects if he doesn't improve. Please call me so we can arrange for a conference to see how we can help him do better in school.

Sincerely,
Mrs. Bolton
5th Grade Teacher

Mom expected that Toby would have problems this year in school because he always had in past school years, but she didn't realize it was going to be this bad. When she saw how upset Toby looked she felt more sorry for him than angry. She said, "Toby, I'm going to call your teacher tomorrow and schedule a conference. I don't know exactly how to help you improve, but maybe Mrs. Bolton can give us some ideas. Now let's get your homework done for starters. Then after dinner you and

I will hit the books."

Toby felt very relieved. Mom didn't seem mad at all. She understood how he was feeling. She knew he really wanted to improve. He just didn't know how. Maybe Mom and Mrs. Bolton could help him.

Mike and May talked all through dinner. May told them about her class play and Mike talked about his upcoming basketball game. Mom was troubled, but tried not to let on. Toby just sat quietly and listened as dinner slowly disappeared.

Chapter
Four

The conference with Toby's teachers was scheduled at school one week later. Mrs. Bolton dismissed the class at the end of the school day. Toby waited in the classroom for her to put away her papers, then together they walked downstairs to the administration offices. As Toby and Mrs. Bolton exited the stairwell, they saw May sitting on the visitors' bench in the main office. May was to wait for Mom and Toby so she didn't have to walk home alone.

May greeted Toby and Mrs. Bolton when she saw them coming. Mrs. Bolton smiled and continued into the guidance counselor's office. Toby stayed with May. He was scared and May tried to help him relax. May whispered, "Don't be nervous Toby. They're just going to try and help you do better."

Inside the conference room at an oval table sat Mrs. Bolton, Toby's teacher, Mr. Sachs, the physical education teacher, and Mrs. Hart, the guidance counselor. The three educators made up Toby's child study team. Toby could hear them introducing themselves to his mother.

Mrs. Hart walked to the doorway and invited Toby to come inside. He didn't want to leave May, but she encouraged him to go. May said she had homework to keep her busy while she waited. Toby entered the room and Mrs. Hart closed the door.

When he entered the conference room Toby's eyes searched for his mother. The teachers smiled and asked him to sit with them at the table so he could be part of the discussion. Toby glanced at Mom. She looked as nervous as he felt.

Mrs. Hart looked at Toby and spoke first. She said that although Toby had some problems in school he should not feel discouraged. She continued by saying, "Anyone who has this many people interested in helping him is bound to do well." Mrs. Bolton took out the letter that she had sent to Toby's mother and spoke about some of the difficulties Toby was having in school with paying attention, staying organized, and finishing his work. Mrs. Hart and Mr. Sachs agreed that Toby showed weakness in the same areas when he was with them. Mrs. Hart explained that each of Toby's teachers had filled out a form which described Toby's work habits in class. All the teachers seemed to agree with one another that Toby was having problems.

BEHAVIOR RATING SCALE

Name __*Toby Butler*__ Grade __5__

Rate the student on each of the following:

	Not At all	Just a Little	Pretty Much	Very Much
1. Has trouble paying attention				✓
2. Cannot concentrate on assigned work			✓	
3. Impulsive; impatient			✓	
4. Difficulty keeping work organized			✓	
5. Has trouble sitting still; fidgets				✓
6. Difficulty finishing work			✓	
7. Tries hard to solve difficult work			✓	
8. Starts fights with others	✓			
9. Short attention span				✓
10. Gets upset easily		✓		

Mrs. Hart spoke again. She told Mrs. Butler that she had reviewed Toby's school records for the past few years and it looked as if he had similar problems before. All the teachers had agreed that Toby tried his best in school, but he just seemed unable to control himself and pay attention.

Mrs. Hart suggested that Toby might have an attention problem known as attention deficit disorder or ADD. To be certain of this being the problem they suggested that Toby meet with a psychologist at school for further evaluation. Mrs. Butler also thought this was a good idea and she and Toby agreed to meet with Dr. Stevens, the school psychologist. Mrs. Hart said she would schedule an appointment with Dr. Stevens and would let Toby and her know when it would be. Dr. Stevens would be a member of Toby's child study team and they would all meet again to discuss the results after the evaluation was completed.

In the meantime, Mrs. Bolton said she knew Toby could do better with some help and she would be willing to help in any way she could. Mr. Sachs remembered that Toby loved to play basketball. He knew Toby's brother, Mike, when he was in his class here at Liberty and knew that he went on to be a star player in high school. Mr. Sachs offered to give Toby some extra time to play basketball during physical education class as a reward for trying harder. Toby liked that idea. He never thought Mr. Sachs would want to help him or give him any special attention. He always thought Mr. Sachs was annoyed with him. Toby felt like all his teachers were trying to help him.

When the conference was over Mom and Toby saw May on the bench with her books back in her book bag, all ready to go.

"May, I'm sorry you had to wait so long, but I think it was worthwhile for us to be here." Mom said.

May replied, "I'm happy, because I got to finish all of my homework."

Chapter
Five

Next week Toby had a new letter in his book bag. This letter was given to him by Mrs. Hart, the guidance counselor. He wasn't scared this time, because when Mrs. Hart brought it to his classroom, Mrs. Bolton, his teacher, gave him a reassuring smile. Even though he wasn't scared, he sure was curious, but he didn't dare to open the letter. He just gave it to his mother when she got home from work.

Mom opened it quickly. This time she did not assume it was just another notice from school. She read the letter and told Toby it was from Mrs. Hart advising them that an appointment had been scheduled for him with Dr. Stevens, the school psychologist.

Toby wanted to know when he was going to see Dr. Stevens and what it would be like. Mom read on and told him that he would be called for in his classroom tomorrow morning. Mrs. Butler was asked to come to school late in the afternoon to meet with Dr. Stevens.

Toby asked his mother if he should prepare for this evaluation. Mom said, "No, Toby, just go and be yourself and do whatever Dr. Stevens asks you to do. They all want to help you." She continued by saying, "I'm just as curious about my interview with him." That made Toby feel a little bit more comfortable with his feelings of uncertainty, but not so eager for this appointment.

The next morning Mrs. Hart called for Toby in class. Toby went down to the guidance office. Although he felt a little nervous, he forced himself to hide it. Mrs. Hart introduced him to Dr. Stevens. The psychologist had a kind face and greeted Toby with a warm, friendly smile.

Dr. Stevens was very friendly. He told Toby that although they were meeting for the first time, he felt like he already knew him. He had already spoken to his teachers about him and had looked over the questionnaires that his teachers had filled out. This helped him see just what kind of problems Toby was having.

Toby and Dr. Stevens talked for a long time. He asked him about Mike and May and his friends at school. He tried to understand the things that Toby liked and didn't like about school and the types of problems he was having in class. Toby found it easy to talk to Dr. Stevens. He seemed to understand just what Toby was going through.

After they talked, Dr. Stevens gave him a bunch of tests. Toby had his memory tested. He put puzzles together, copied drawings, answered a lot of questions and he even got to take a test on a computer. This evaluation thing wasn't so bad at all. Toby was enjoying it. He really liked talking to Dr. Stevens.

After two or three hours of work, including a lunch break during which Toby was able to go back to the lunchroom and eat with his classmates, the evaluation was over. Toby thanked Dr. Stevens and told him he had fun. Dr. Stevens said he did too and that Toby had cooperated and had done a great job. Dr. Stevens said that he looked forward to meeting Toby's mother later in the day.

Mrs. Hart met Mrs. Butler in the guidance office and introduced her to Dr. Stevens. He asked her a lot of questions about Toby and how he got along at home now and in the past. Mrs. Butler explained that Toby's father had died a few years ago and since then she had looked after the three children by herself. Mike and May were easy to manage, but Toby always seemed to have a harder time with paying attention and settling down, especially in school. They talked for a long time and after filling out a questionnaire about Toby, she was finished.

Dr. Stevens told Mrs. Butler that he would write a report on his findings after which he would meet with her, Toby and the other members of the child study team. At this meeting he would review the results and make some recommendations. Mrs. Butler was anxious to know the results.

Chapter
Six

A few days later Mike, May, Toby and Mom sat around the kitchen table and had a delicious breakfast of pancakes and sausages. It wasn't often that they enjoyed a feast like this on a weekday morning. Mike tried to prepare good breakfasts, but he just couldn't cook like Mom.

Later that morning, Mom and Toby were scheduled to visit his school and meet with his child study team. Dr. Stevens had prepared the results of the evaluation. At this meeting they would be explained. Toby and Mom weren't so nervous this time. They were very eager to hear the results and they felt very relaxed about talking with the child study team.

When they entered the room Mr. Sachs, Mrs. Bolton and Mrs. Hart were already seated. Mrs. Hart broke the ice by saying, "Now, all we need is Dr. Stevens!" Everyone smiled and Toby and Mom felt welcomed. In walked Dr. Stevens. They all exchanged greetings and the meeting began.

certainly be able to earn this extra time. He even imagined playing for the school team when he got older like his brother.

Mrs. Bolton spoke next, interrupting Toby's thoughts about basketball. She said she would try to help Toby by dividing up his work into shorter assignments. Toby would be given a new seat in the front of the class and every time Mrs. Bolton gave a homework assignment she would write it on the chalkboard and give Toby plenty of time to copy it. She would even make a point of checking Toby's work as he completed it and would help him keep his notebook organized. To encourage him to use more self-control she would give him extra credit for raising his hand and waiting to be called on. He would lose credit points if he called out. Toby thought that sounded pretty easy to follow. He felt good about having the opportunity to earn extra credit. He had never really thought about that before. Mike and May boasted lots of times about getting extra credit in class.

Mrs. Hart said she would help by meeting with Toby regularly and talking to him about his progress. She gave him a special student planbook. This book would help him keep his work organized. He could write his assignments in the planbook and check them off as he completed them. It even had a section for his teachers to rate him each day. Mom could look at it after school so she could keep up with his progress too.

Daily Record Form

| Name: | Day: | Date: |

Subjects	Homework Assignments	Due	Supplies Needed
English			
Math			
Social Studies			
Science			

Today's Homework

Are all assignments copied?   Teacher's initials:

Classroom Performance Ratings
(Select frequency of ratings per day: AM, PM, All Day, or by Subject)

	AM	PM	All Day	Eng.	Math	Soc. Stud.	Sci.	Other
Paid attention in class								
Completed work in class								
Completed homework								
Was well behaved								
Work neat and organized								
Other_____								
Total Number Points Earned								
Teacher's Initials								

Score Board

Parent's Signature:
Comments:

Points: 1 = Poor; 2 = Needs Improvement;
3 = Fair; 4 = Good; 5= Excellent;
0 = No form returned; NA = Not Applicable

This sounded very promising to Toby. Now, he could finally schedule himself to get his work done. Mike always told him that the reason he never finished anything was because he didn't stay on a schedule. All he needed was a little help and this planbook might just do the trick.

Before the meeting ended, Dr. Stevens mentioned that there was yet another way to manage ADD. He said that some youngsters took medication which improved their concentration. Kids found it easier to pay attention and complete assignments without becoming distracted when they took the medication. He recommended to Mrs. Butler that she contact Toby's doctor to find out if he thought Toby could benefit by taking medication. Mrs. Butler agreed to bring Toby to her hospital clinic so they could find out more about medications for ADD.

Chapter
Seven

Several months had passed since Mom and Toby had the meeting with the child study team. Things had changed quite a bit for Toby. He was finishing his work in class and wasn't getting into as much trouble as he had before. He felt better about himself and his schoolwork.

Going to school in the morning was even getting to be fun. Now, when he was in the school yard, the guys invited him to shoot hoops. He always made sure to wait his turn before taking the ball. He remembered how upset Carl had become when he took his turn away.

Carl turned out to be a nice guy. He and Toby started eating lunch together. Toby asked Carl why they didn't become friends sooner.

Carl said, "Toby, you were hard to be friends with. You never listened when anyone talked to you and you interrupted a lot."

Toby said, "I never knew I did that, Carl."

"Well, it doesn't matter. We're friends now and that's okay." replied Carl.

At first Mrs. Butler was reluctant to give Toby medication, but the doctor at the clinic said many children do very well with it. He examined Toby, looked at the rating scales that his teachers had filled out, and read the results of Dr. Stevens' evaluation. He told Mrs. Butler and Toby he agreed with Dr. Stevens. Toby had ADD.

The doctor explained that many children who have ADD can be helped by certain medicine that can improve their concentration. He explained that if the medicine were to work, Toby would have to take it at least once a day.

Mom wanted to give the medicine a try and now Toby was glad she did. When he took the medicine, Toby didn't feel as restless. He seemed to get all his work done in school instead of wasting time. Perhaps the medicine was helping him.

School work seemed easier now. Well, maybe it was just because Toby was prepared.

Mrs. Bolton really tried to be helpful. She hardly ever scolded Toby anymore. He even thought that she liked him.

Toby made a special effort to do a good job with his student planbook. He made sure to list all of his assignments and complete them. He really took pride when he got a good rating from his teachers. It was especially nice at dinnertime when he showed it to his mother.

Toby was pleased about the way things were working out at home. Mom was never on his case about the mornings anymore. That was probably because he and Mike wrote out a schedule and a checklist for the morning. Toby kept up with it and everything was going right.

He still checked on May in the mornings and

helped her get off to school. May liked having Toby give her that attention. But the most important thing was that Toby helped himself. He got himself off to school on time and left home prepared for the day.

Mike was really proud of him. He even invited Toby to practice basketball with him at Kennedy High. Mike never used to like having Toby around for that, but he didn't seem to mind anymore.

Mr. Sachs rewarded Toby whenever he followed instructions in physical education class. He got so much extra time to shoot baskets that he was becoming an even better player. Mr. Sachs said it was because he was concentrating more, and maybe one day he would play like Mike.

Today was going to be a special day. May's class was going to do a play for the entire school. Mom was on her way so she could see it too. Toby, Mom, and Mike were all so happy for May. After lunch, Toby's class went out to the school yard until the multi-purpose lunch room could be set up for the play.

Mrs. Bolton said the boys and girls could shoot hoops while they waited. The kids decided to split up into two teams and play for points. This made things a lot more exciting. Carl and Toby were on the same team. They knew their competition was fierce. Some really good players were on the other team, but Carl and Toby were confident they could win.

They played hard and Toby must have been fo-
cused, because whenever the ball came to him he got a
basket. As the ball went through the hoop, his team-
mates cheered for him and called out, "Slam dunk!"

When the game was over Toby's team had won and
all the kids cheered. They called him, "Toby the Slam
Dunk Man." It really felt good to have friends. Toby
beamed.

As he looked up he saw Mom. She said,
"Congratulations, son! I'm really proud of you."

That felt even better. Just like a slam dunk.

Commonly Asked Questions About Attention Deficit Disorder by Harvey C. Parker, Ph.D.

1. What is attention deficit disorder (ADD)?

ADD is a biological disorder which affects a person's ability to pay attention. Those with ADD usually have trouble concen-trating and at times trouble controlling their behavior. Some individuals with ADD can not sit still for long periods of time without getting rest-less and fidgety and, in turn, are frequently per-ceived as hyperactive.  Others with ADD are exactly the opposite. While they also have trouble paying attention, they are not consid-ered hyperactive. In fact, they seem to be less active than most and usually take longer to get things done.

ADD can effect a person's life in many ways. It can hinder performance in school, make it difficult to make as well as keep friends, and cause problems at home. Having ADD is no one's fault! With help from parents and teachers and a lot of effort, a person can overcome some of the problems that ADD might cause. Remember, no one is responsible for causing ADD, but if a person has ADD they are responsible for trying to control it.

2. What causes a person to have ADD?

Although no one is sure what exactly causes an attention deficit disorder, some scientists believe it has something to do with the way the body works to control behavior and attention. The brain is a complex information network made up of billions of nerve cells called neurons. Neurons send information to each other in much the same way as signals are transmitted electronically in a telecommunica-

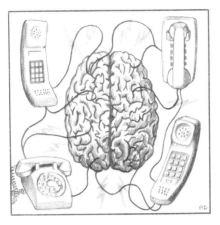

tions network. However, messages within the brain are transferred by substances called neurotransmitter chemicals. People with ADD may not have enough of these chemicals and, therefore, their body has trouble controlling attention and activity.

3. Is ADD inherited?

In some cases, probably yes. Like the color of one's eyes or hair, ADD has been thought to be hereditary. Therefore, most people with ADD were probably born with it. If a person has ADD, there is a high probability that a biological relative has suffered as well from the same condition. Since ADD tends to be more common in boys than in girls, ask some of your male relatives if they ever had trouble paying attention.

4. How else can a person get ADD?

We are not sure of all the ways a person can get ADD. We do know that it isn't contagious, so you can't catch it from someone else. We also know that those who have ADD were probably born with it, unless they had an accident or illness, which could have affected the way their body is able to pay attention and manage their impulses and activity.

5. Does diet make a difference?

That is a rather difficult question to answer and one which many people have argued about for several years. Some scientists believe there is a relationship between what people eat and how they act. They blame certain types of food such as sugar, artificial colorings and preservatives for causing hyperactivity. However, other scientists studied children on many different kinds of diets to see what affect, if any, food would have on behavior. The results seemed to indicate that food has little affect on behavior and for most people it does not cause ADD.   Needless to say, however, if a person has ADD it is a good rule of thumb for them to avoid eating foods which seem to affect their attention span or behavior.

6. Why does a person have to take medication if they have ADD?

They don't! Taking medication for any illness or condition is a personal decision that obviously requires a great deal of thought along with input from both a physician and one's parents. Keep in mind that for most children and teenagers with ADD, taking medication has been found to help them pay attention, control behavior, and perform more effectively in school. On the other hand, there are those who feel that medication should only be taken when you are sick. Since ADD doesn't make a person feel sick, they do not see the point in taking medication.

Nevertheless, the various medications used to manage ADD have proven to be of enormous benefit because they somehow affect chemicals in the body that help one to pay attention and stay in control. Still, even though it helps to correct a problem, putting something in one's body to effect the way the body reacts is not something a person should do without giving it a great deal of thought.

7. How can medication help?

There are several different kinds of medication that can help children, teens and even adults who have ADD. The most commonly prescribed is Ritalin. When a person with ADD takes Ritalin they often do better in school and on tasks which require them to pay attention. Ritalin reduces hyperactivity and helps control behavior so the person will more likely think things through before reacting.

Since Ritalin improves attention span and helps hyperactive children settle down, teachers often find that ADD students who take Ritalin get more of their work done in school and listen better.

8. What are the side-effects of Ritalin?

Side-effects are the unwanted effects that medication produces in your body. They can sometimes be quite uncomfortable and that is one of the reasons we try to

it sometimes improves by itself as the person gets older. For instance, young ADD children often have more trouble sitting still and paying attention than do teenagers. Therefore, teenagers can sometimes take less medicine than a younger child might need. Most children who take medicine to manage their attention deficit disorder will use the medicine for several years and maybe longer if they find it helpful. It has recently been discovered that adults who have ADD can be helped by the same medicines that children take.

12. Are there any benefits to having ADD?

Although having ADD can cause many problems, there may be some advantages as well. Many children with ADD have excellent memories for past events that others tend to forget. Hyperactive people are energetic and if they put their energy to good use they can accomplish a lot in a short period of time. Many adults with hyperactivity are quite successful. They never seem to "run out of steam" and can handle several different tasks at the same time. In fact, they are fun to be around and others tend to find them exciting and interesting.

13. How does having an attention deficit disorder affect a person in school?

ADD can cause significant problems in school. For instance, since children with ADD have trouble paying attention and keeping their mind on their work, they often have to be reminded to listen and to stay on task. More often than not, they have trouble completing their work. Some ADD children who are hyperactive also have trouble sitting still for an entire class period and they find themselves getting restless and fidgety. Further problems result from their impulsivity (excitability and impatience) and resultant tendency to rush through assignments without due care for the neatness or accuracy of their answers. Those with ADD have to try harder in school than others do. They have to remind themselves to pay attention and to be careful when doing their work.

14. How can a student with ADD pay better attention in class?

The first step is to try harder to concentrate. Concentration is an active not a passive process. Maintaining alertness in class can be achieved by following some of these suggestions:
- participate in class discussions
- ask questions when not understanding something
- take notes
- look at the teacher
- do homework the night before so you'll feel involved
- listen to what's going on
- sit near the teacher
- break the daydreaming habit
- try to model other students who are paying attention

15. How can I develop better study skills?

Developing good study skills is a key to success in school. Try to get into the routine of following these suggestions.

1. Find the best time for you to study. Do it when you are best able to concentrate and when your mind is most receptive to learning information. Some people retain information better when they study at night while others do better in the afternoon or early mornings. Find a comfortable place for studying and use it regularly. The same desk creates familiarity and helps in getting started each time.

2. Set realistic goals. For example, don't force yourself to read an entire chapter in your biology book if your concentration can't last that long. Read what you can, take a break, and read some more later. If you have work to do in several subjects, estimate how long you will need to spend on each assignment.

3. Preview selections or whole chapters in textbooks before reading for details. Move quickly through a chapter skimming much faster than your usual reading rate. The goal is to get an overview of what is important and how the information is presented. Notice all bold-face headings and subheadings. Scan maps, diagrams and illustrations. This should only take a few seconds per page.

4. Read the chapter for the purpose of understanding the material, not to memorize details. Write down

information that you want to remember later. It is important to continually write down such summaries of what you are reading. Get into the habit of reading and writing so you are actively doing something with the information you read.

5. Once you've read the chapter and have taken notes, take a short break. Then go through the chapter and skim it again slowly to refresh your memory. Answer chapter questions. Make sure you have a good understanding of the material. Fill in your notes with additional information you determine to be important.

6. Now put this information into memory. Every once in a while use visualization to remember details. While seated, close your eyes and picture a blank screen in your mind. Picture details of what you want to remember on the mental screen. Focus on the main points. Let the visual image "sink" into your mind. Repeat important statements to yourself and then repeat them out loud. Practice recalling information with and without referring to your notes.

7. Don't just study when you have a test. Reviewing material nightly will make it easier to remember information later in preparation for testing.

16. How can I keep my mind on my homework?

Finding a quiet place at home to work and break-

ing your assignments down into smaller parts sometimes helps.

1. If there is a page or more of problems to do, try
    dividing the assignment into three or four sec-
    tions.
2. Spend ten or fifteen minutes on each section.
    Keep a clock or timer nearby so as to keep track
    of the time.
3. Stop working when the time is up or if you com-
    plete the section.
4. Take a break before using the same procedure
    with the next section of work.

17. How can I keep friends?

The best way to keep a friend is to be a friend.
While there is no simple formula for making friends or
keeping them, here are a few suggestions that might be
useful.

- A good friend shows caring. Everybody likes to be cared about and when a person shows someone that he/she cares for them they tend to be liked more. There are a lot of ways to show  people you care about them: talking to someone shows care; asking how they are shows care; taking an interest in what they do shows care; going places with them and doing things together shows care.

- A good friend avoids arguments and tries not to blame others. While it is not necessary to agree with everything everyone says or does, it is important to disagree with others in a way which doesn't hurt somebody's feelings.

- A good friend keeps promises. People who say they are going to do one thing and end up doing another usually do not make great friends. People usually think of them as phonies and do not trust them in the future.

- A good friend recognizes that people sometimes need space and gives it to them. Probably one of the biggest problems that ADD children have in keeping friends is that they overwhelm others. This is easy to do when hyperactive. Hyperactivity can cause someone to be too excitable, too opinionated, too bossy, or too impatient with others. Needless to say, most friends won't be too happy about that and will probably want to have contact in small doses only. If one is coming on too strong, take a step back, calm down and start all over again.

- A good friend takes an interest in what others like. People tend to make friends with others who share common interests. Finding out what a person likes to do is a good way to start conversations and can help when plans are made to get together with one another.

18. How can I be less impulsive?

Psychologists have developed methods to help ADD children "stop and think" before reacting too quickly to a situation. Finding a well thought out solution to a problem, putting that solution into action, and evaluating the success of your behavior requires some advanced planning. Try following these five problem solving steps the next time you face a problem.

Step 1: Ask yourself, what is the problem?

Step 2: Ask yourself, what are some plans I can use to solve the problem?

Step 3: Pick the best plan.

Step 4: Try the plan out.

Step 5: Ask yourself, did the plan work?

It is quite important to think through problems rather than make quick decisions.

19. Can I expect my attention span to improve as I get older?

Yes, you probably can. Experts have studied teenagers with ADD and have followed them as they became adults. They have found that for many people, problems with attention span, hyperactivity, and impulsiveness (impatience) lessen with time.

By all means, remember that having attention deficit disorder is not the "end of the world." You can still succeed in school, go to college if you like, and be successful in your career, even with ADD. It might cause you some trouble here and there, but there's a lot you can do to help yourself succeed.

20. Where can a person find more information on ADD?

CH.A.D.D., Children and Adults with Attention Deficit Disorders, is a national ADD support group. CH.A.D.D. maintains several hundred chapters across the country which provide support and information to families and professionals. Write or call for information:

CH.A.D.D.

499 Northwest 70th Avenue

Plantation, Florida 33317

(305) 587-3700